SUPER DC HEROES

BATMAN

ARCTIC ATTACK

WRITTEN BY
ROBERT GREENBERGER

ILLUSTRATED BY
JASON KRUSE AND
LEE LOUGHRIDGE

BATMAN CREATED BY
BOB KANE

STONE ARCH BOOKS
MINNEAPOLIS   SAN DIEGO

Published by Stone Arch Books in 2010
151 Good Counsel Drive, P.O. Box 669
Mankato, Minnesota 56002
www.stonearchbooks.com

Library of Congress Cataloging-in-Publication Data

Greenberger, Robert.
  Arctic attack / by Robert Greenberger ; illustrated by Jason Kruse.
    p. cm. -- (DC super heroes. Batman)
  ISBN 978-1-4342-1561-1 (lib. bdg.) -- ISBN 978-1-4342-1728-8 (pbk.)
  [1. Superheroes--Fiction.] I. Kruse, Jason T., ill. II. Title.
  PZ7.G82764Ar 2010
  [Fic]--dc22
                              2009008735

Summary: While researching the Arctic for a school project, Robin
discovers that something is heating the glaciers — and it's not just global
warming. With Batman's help, Robin discovers that the evil Rā's al Ghūl
is behind the environmental disruption. The Dynamic Duo head to the
Arctic to stop his evil plan and prevent an ecological disaster.

Art Director: Bob Lentz
Designer: Brann Garvey

TABLE OF CONTENTS

CHAPTER 1

THE BATCAVE

Below Wayne Manor rests the vast cavern known as the Batcave. It is equipped with the most amazing collection of tools and equipment. The tools were created by Batman to help him in his war on crime. They give him instant access to information from all over the world.

One evening, instead of using the Batcave's powerful computer to track criminals, Tim Drake was using it to finish his homework. The teen munched on some popcorn as he worked.

Tim's focus was broken as the deep rumble from the Batmobile's powerful engine echoed throughout the cave. The sleek car slid into place behind where Tim was sitting.

The dark figure of Batman leaped out of the car and walked toward Tim. The crime fighter took off his mask and set it on the computer table.

"Back so soon?" Tim asked.

"Quiet night," Batman answered. His low growl echoed through the cave.

Batman studied the screen. Then he looked at Tim's notebook. "What's the assignment?" he asked.

"I have to do a report on global warming and its effect on the North Pole," Tim replied.

Batman nodded. He began to walk away from the computer, but then he paused. He turned quickly, his cape rustling behind him. The Dark Knight studied the screen one more time.

"Where is this data coming from?" Batman asked his adopted son.

"It's from the International Arctic Buoy Program," Tim answered. "It's a string of 700 buoys located throughout the Arctic Ocean. They provide readings of the temperatures there."

"Hmm," Batman said, looking puzzled. "The temperature readings are higher than they should be."

"How did you know that?" Tim asked, his eyes wide with surprise.

"It's right in front of us," Batman said.

Batman's gloved hand pointed to a set of numbers on the screen. "Given the time of year, the position of the sun, and the average temperatures for the region around Greenland, the temperature is rising too fast. It's not noticeable to most observers," Batman said.

"Unless you know what to look for," Tim said, smiling.

The teen closed his notebook. "Could it be the greenhouse effect working faster than expected?" Tim asked, straightening up in his chair.

"Scientists have been watching the area for some time now," Batman replied. "This is an unusual set of readings going back a week. Nothing has changed in the atmosphere or local environment to explain this change."

"So you think the temperature spike is unnatural?" Tim asked.

"Yes, I think it's man-made," Batman said. He began to type on the keyboard.

"If the speed of the temperature climb remains steady, then in just a few weeks, enough ice will have melted to cause major problems," Batman said. He pointed to the screen that showed a map of the Northern Hemisphere.

"What kinds of problems?" Tim asked.

"The softening ice," Batman answered, his finger identifying the coast of Canada. "It could crack and fall into the Arctic Ocean. The icebergs could threaten ships by blocking the shipping lanes. This also means the native species up there will have less land to live on."

"It will also be warmer than the animals are used to," Batman said. "That will put them in danger as well."

"I wonder what's causing it," Tim said.

Batman studied the screen. He slowly nodded his head. Finally, he said, "The buoys use electronic sensors to measure temperatures. It looks like someone has been using the sensors as intense heat rays instead."

Tim said, "Wow! Is that possible?"

"Only the most sophisticated mind could have planned this deadly scheme," Batman said. "Who would benefit from raising the sea level and threatening life around the world?"

Tim's fingers quickly keyed a name into the computer. "Rā's al Ghūl," he said.

"I agree," Batman replied. He glared at the picture of the villain on the computer screen. "Rā's is an ecoterrorist. He's trying to restore the world to its pristine condition before man started burning fossil fuels. It's definitely his style."

Batman turned and walked toward one of the cabinets in the Batcave. He removed two special backpacks and outfits from inside.

"I think we need to investigate in person," Batman said to Robin.

FLAP! Tim slammed his notebook shut. "Field trip!" he said.

"If this is Rā's al Ghūl's doing, then you need to be ready," Batman warned the teen. "Pack your gear. I'll prepare the Batplane."

CHAPTER 2

INTO THE ARCTIC

The Batplane lifted off the ground. It rushed through a maze of tunnels that connected the Batcave to a cliff overlooking a bay. The bat-shaped jet burst through the cliff and into the air. Then it climbed swiftly into the sky.

Inside the cockpit, the Dynamic Duo adjusted their controls. They spoke using headsets in their masks. The jet's engines were among the fastest ones ever built. They would get the heroes to the Arctic in just a few hours.

"Tell me what you know about the Arctic zone," Batman insisted.

Robin frowned. "I thought homework time was over," he said.

"We have to be prepared for the streets or rooftops or even snow banks," Batman explained.

Robin nodded. He thought for a moment before answering. "In addition to our destination, Greenland, the zone includes Canada, Finland, Iceland, Norway, Russia, and Sweden," he said.

"You forgot Alaska," Batman added.

"Sorry," Robin said. "The zone countries do research and share information." He adjusted a control on his side of the cockpit. Then he reached below his seat where a small cooler held bottled water.

Robin drank a big gulp of water before he was asked the next question.

"Good. Now, how do we find Rā's al Ghūl?" Batman asked.

That question made Robin pause. He rested his chin on a gloved hand. Batman adjusted the Batplane's controls and waited patiently for an answer.

Rā's al Ghūl had lived for centuries. He renewed his life over and over by bathing in the chemical pools known as the Lazarus Pits. In his mind, the world had grown too full over the years. It could not support six billion people. So, he had dedicated himself to reducing the population.

Rā's al Ghūl could spend decades on each scheme. His long lifespan allowed him time to outlive his enemies.

Only Batman had managed to end the ecoterrorist's plans before they could be completed. Even with help from the League of Assassins, Rā's had failed each time.

But Rā's seemed to enjoy his fights with Batman. After their first meeting, Rā's believed that Batman was his equal. He thought the Caped Crusader was someone who could be his successor someday. Batman had rejected the offer, knowing that Rā's wanted to wipe out most of the life on Earth.

"We know Rā's al Ghūl is altering the buoy system to use them as heat rays," Batman said.

"So we use the buoys to find him," Robin said.

"Exactly," answered Batman.

With that, Batman activated the onboard systems. They were linked to the giant computer mainframe back at the Batcave. **CLICK!** He pressed a button and watched a small screen blink to life. A map appeared that was covered with red dots. The dots showed the positions of the 700 buoys. Moments later, several of the red dots turned blue and began to move. When they stopped, they were in a straight line across the Arctic Ocean.

"You found him already?" Robin asked, surprised.

Batman grinned. "It helps when you know what you're looking for," he said. "The signal begins in Greenland and then runs north. It melts everything in its path faster than the surrounding water can absorb it."

"So now we just land and grab him?" Robin asked.

"Something like that," Batman said with a smile. He was clearly planning the next move.

Robin also fell silent. But his thoughts were about the melting ice, not the villain. "Can the melting ice also harm Gotham City?" he asked.

Batman replied, "Over the next century, the sea level could rise two inches."

"That's not enough to hurt the city," Robin interrupted.

"No, it isn't," Batman agreed. "But it can be enough to start a chain reaction. The warming air could lead to ice disappearing entirely from many of these Arctic zone countries."

Batman continued, "The melting ice could even release gases or diseases that have been trapped for centuries beneath the ice."

"Ice is melting all over the world, too. So a little bit can start to add up very quickly," continued Batman.

"Polar bears, and many other species, are endangered for many of the same reasons," Robin added.

Batman adjusted the Batplane as it began its descent toward the cold, hard land. The tundra beneath them looked harsh and uninviting.

Batman turned from the controls and looked Robin straight in the eyes. "It's not just the animals that are in danger," Batman said.

"Rā's wants to eliminate mankind. He also wants to remake the world as he sees fit," Batman said. "But he can't predict what kind of deadly effect that his plans could have on Earth."

Robin looked up at his partner and nodded. "And that's why Rā's has to be stopped," he said.

CHAPTER 3

HUNTING BY LAND

WHOOOOSH! The arctic wind whipped against the Batplane. The powerful jet touched down on a remote stretch of snowy land. After they shut off the engines, Batman and Robin walked toward the rear of the jet.

First, they stopped to put on some high-tech gloves. They were insulated to keep them warm in the harsh arctic climate. Special gray-colored capes were designed to help them blend in with the landscape.

CLICK! They activated their radios inside the earholes of their masks. Now they could communicate by radio.

Batman flipped a switch on the Batplane, lowering a rear panel. **CLICK!** He pressed a button that lowered a ramp to the ground.

As the ramp touched down on the snow, the Dynamic Duo climbed aboard two snowmobiles. They were specially made vehicles with reduced engine noise. They let the heroes travel swiftly and quietly.

Batman flipped up a small screen on his dashboard that displayed a map of the area. A blinking light showed the source of the energy. If Batman was right, that was where the villain would be found. The Dark Knight pointed toward their right. Then he turned on his snowmobile's engine.

The rear tracks of the snowmobile hummed to life. They gripped the hard snow and ice. Quickly and quietly, the twin snowmobiles sped away.

Robin took a quick look over his shoulder. The ramp had retracted back inside the plane, and the doors had closed. It was safely sealed shut.

This was Robin's first time in the Arctic. He allowed himself a chance to admire the beautiful, desolate scenery. The land was rough, but not absent of life. Short grass, small plants, and even moss grew in many places. In the distance, he spotted a herd of caribou.

"I hope you're finished sightseeing," Batman warned over his radio headset.

"Remember, Rā's al Ghūl is extremely dangerous," Batman said.

"I know," Robin sighed. "We've fought him in Gotham many times."

"This isn't Gotham," Batman said. "He is likely to have his assassins protecting him. And his personal bodyguard, Ubu, will probably be close by, too."

"We've stopped him before, and we'll stop him this time," Robin said. "Being in the Arctic is cool, but it's just another crime we're stopping."

Robin liked that they were getting closer to the herd of caribou. He'd never seen any before. One of them was nibbling on a low plant.

"It's more serious than that," Batman explained.

"If he succeeds this time," Batman said, "he will start a chain reaction that we may not be able to stop. It's not just Gotham that's at risk. The entire world is in danger, Robin."

Robin swallowed hard. Now he realized what was at stake. The wind rushed inside his hood, chilling his ears. He shivered, but it wasn't because of the cold.

"His goals are admirable, but he is short-sighted," Batman said. "He refuses to think we can solve the problems that previous generations created."

BZZT! Suddenly, ruby-red lights sprang to life from beneath piles of ice and rock. Laser beams, designed to melt through the frozen rock and tundra, shot straight toward Robin's snowmobile.

Robin watched a beam cut into the ground in front of him. Dirt and rocks flew into the air. They created a dirty fog as the cut in the ground grew larger. He was surprised by a loud **RUMMMMMMBLE!** as the ground split apart. Robin jerked on the handles of his snowmobile and skidded to his left. He was trying to circle around the beams and the cracks in the ground.

If the lasers hit, the snowmobiles would be destroyed. The two heroes would be stranded in the middle of nowhere.

BIZZIT! Another set of lasers sprang upward. Batman's hands pulled the machine to his right, leaning into a turn. His weight helped tip the speeding vehicle on its side, lifting one set of tracks into the air. This turned the machine sharply to avoid the super-hot beams.

Batman returned to his original path toward a brown hill that was dotted with snow. Robin lined himself up with Batman's new heading.

Bright sunlight reflected off something high on the hill. Batman made a quick hand gesture, directing Robin to move off in a different direction. Batman then turned in the opposite direction and heard a high whistling sound.

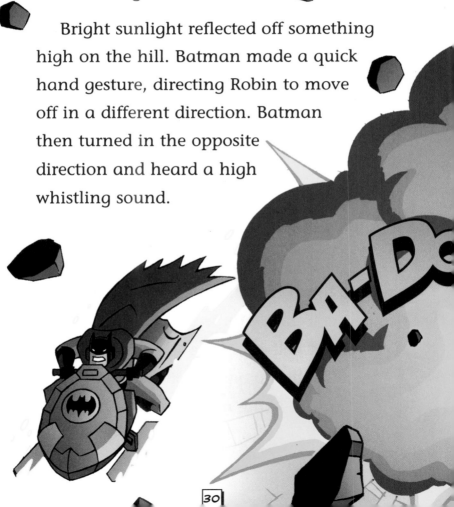

The ground shook violently. Robin nearly lost his grip on the handlebars. A small missile had hit the tundra. It had carved a deep hole where the two snowmobiles had been just moments before.

CHAPTER 4

INTO THE VILLAIN'S LAIR

The laser attacks on the snowmobiles stopped after the missile struck. Batman pointed to a nearby hill. There was a dark opening in its side.

Batman and Robin parked their snowmobiles at the side of the mound. Then they locked the controls.

After glancing around the quiet area, Batman saw that no one else was outside. He and Robin began walking toward the gap in the hill. They moved with firm, silent steps across the snow.

The opening in the hill was dark, but their special goggles allowed them to see in the shadows. After a few minutes of walking, they felt the cool air get warmer. The sides of the tunnel were smooth. That meant machines had dug them.

Farther ahead, they heard electronic sounds. It sounded like the computers in the Batcave.

A new sound came from nearby. It was the sound of metal sliding. Someone in the shadows was preparing to fire a weapon.

Batman quickly reached into his Utility Belt and pulled out a Batarang. With ease, he threw it into the darkness. He knew he hit his target when a man yelled in pain.

A second Batarang soon followed. This time a weapon dropped to the ground.

Behind the guard, another assassin was getting his rifle ready to fire. The Dynamic Duo ran forward. They zig-zagged to avoid being easy targets.

As they neared the first guard, Batman lashed out with a punch. **THUD!** The man fell to the icy floor.

Robin rushed past the Dark Knight and jumped high into the air. **SLAM!** His boot connected with the second gunman's chest. The impact knocked the man backward. **BANG!** His gun fired into the tunnel's ceiling.

Robin landed above the man. With a double-handed punch, Robin knocked him out cold.

Loud footsteps echoed in the tunnel. The heroes knew that more men were coming.

Batman removed his special cape, revealing his normal outfit underneath. It was better suited for the dim tunnel, since it let him blend into the shadows. Robin also dropped his winter cape and ran after him.

Before they had gone ten feet, they saw a dozen armed men blocking their path. Batman could see light coming from behind them. It likely came from the area where Rā's al Ghūl worked. The gunmen were simply there to delay the heroes from reaching the villain.

The fight was brief. Batman tossed men over his shoulder. Robin knocked others to the ground. They piled one unconscious man atop the next.

Oomf! Fists cracked against weapons. Boots flew above the ground. Within moments, the guards were no longer able to fight.

Carefully, Batman and Robin made their way to the source of the light. Before entering the large room, Batman paused. He studied it, looking for traps. He saw giant computers, monitors, and one man — Rā's al Ghūl. The villain had his back to them. He was tall and dressed in green and gold. Rā's al Ghūl was focused on the screens, not the men here to stop his plans.

"I have been expecting you, detective!" Rā's al Ghūl said in a smooth voice.

Batman took one step into the large, well-lit room. Suddenly, his left arm was grabbed, and he was tugged off his feet.

CHAPTER 5

FIGHT FOR SURVIVAL

The bald man who was pulling Batman into a bear hug was Ubu, Rā's al Ghūl's guardian. He was nearly seven feet tall and was made entirely of muscle. The tight squeeze made it hard for Batman to move or even breathe.

Robin rushed into the room. He stood between Ubu and Rā's al Ghūl.

As he watched the men struggle, Robin hatched a plan. **CLICK!** He flipped open a compartment in his Utility Belt and quickly fished out a few objects.

Batman stopped struggling, and Ubu gave him one more giant squeeze. At that moment, Batman's heel kicked Ubu's right knee. Ubu staggered backward from the blow. Batman's head smacked against Ubu's face. **WHAM!** Ubu was stunned, and he loosened his grip a little. Batman flexed his powerful muscles and freed himself.

The Dark Knight whirled around and swung his right fist in a circle. As Batman fought against the giant Ubu, the bodyguard crashed into a computer screen. The current zipped through Ubu's body, surrounding him with electricity.

ZZRRRRTT!

Ubu slumped to the ground. He was unconscious.

"Well done, detective," Rā's said.

"You know why I'm here," Batman said to Rā's. The hero moved closer. His footsteps were loud in the large room. They forced Rā's al Ghūl to turn and face him.

Rā's nodded toward Batman in greeting. Then he nodded once at Robin.

When Rā's returned his gaze to Batman, Robin quickly glanced around the room. He was looking for the computer that controlled the buoys.

"You know why I must do this," the villain said. "I have seen what mankind has done to this world. It has to be stopped."

"It's not for you to decide how to change the world," Batman said, moving closer. Batman didn't seem to be in pain, but Robin could see a small cut on his face.

"One man *can* make a difference," Rā's al Ghūl said. "Isn't that what people in America say?"

"Always," Batman answered.

"Then why can't *I* be that man?" Rā's asked.

"You plan to end the lives of billions," Batman said. "That's not a good way to change the world."

"Is someone else doing a better job of saving the planet?" Rā's asked. His left hand inched toward the golden belt he wore.

"Many people are trying to change the health of this planet," Batman said. "They recycle. They use less. They create programs to protect endangered species. There is still hope."

"Too little and too late," the villain said. "What I am doing will bring about a major change. People will either adapt, or they will die."

"You know I can't allow this to happen," Batman said.

With Rā's distracted, Robin attached several small explosives to the computers. He silently thumbed them to life. Then he waited for the right time to strike.

"I think the time for talking is over, detective," Rā's al Ghūl said. He drew a sword from beneath the folds of his robe. It gleamed in the light.

Batman firmly planted his feet, ready for battle. Robin, though, chose that moment to trigger the devices with a remote control attached to his belt. *BOOM!*

The first explosions rocked the room just as Rā's al Ghūl lifted his blade. The air was quickly filled with smoke from the burning computers. Rā's lost his footing and slammed into a table. At that moment, Batman lunged forward to knock the sword from Rā's al Ghūl's hand.

The smoke, though, was growing thick and dark. Batman covered his mouth with a portion of his cape. He reached through the smoke to where he thought Rā's was standing. Instead, his hand grabbed at nothing but air.

FLASH! The entire room was full of sparking electric wires, small fires, and thick smoke.

The Dark Knight couldn't breathe. He was forced to retreat from the smoking room.

Batman backed toward the tunnel. Ubu remained unconscious on the ground. The heroes dragged his body to safety.

Then the Dynamic Duo dashed into the tunnel. They gulped in fresh air. Robin coughed twice as he caught his breath.

Batman placed his hand on the teen's shoulder. "Good work, Robin," Batman said. "The buoys will stop heating the ice and temperatures will return to normal soon."

The two ran down the tunnel, past the bodies of the unconscious guards.

"Will they be safe?" Robin asked, as they ran toward their snowmobiles.

"The smoke will stay at the top of the tunnel," Batman assured him. "They'll be fine."

Soon, they were out of the tunnel and away from the hill. They gunned their snowmobiles to life. **VROOOOM!!**

As they rode back toward the Batplane, the two were quiet for a while.

"Do you think you changed his mind?" Robin asked, breaking the silence.

"I always like to think so," Batman said. "But Rā's al Ghūl has held his beliefs for ages. I doubt he has changed his mind after our little talk."

"Where do you think he went?" Robin asked as the two rode their vehicles onto the Batplane.

"He had an escape route ready, we can be sure of that," the Dark Knight said.

Batman climbed off his snowmobile. He clicked the switch to retract the ramp.

The Dark Knight removed his mask. He looked over at Robin as they activated the Batplane's engines. "You were great out there today, Tim," he said. "Good work."

Robin smiled. It was a rare occasion to receive praise from the Caped Crusader.

"Thanks, Bruce," said Robin.

In silence, the two flew the Batplane back to Gotham City. The heroes would continue to keep the streets of Gotham safe, sharpening their skills and minds. Whatever Rā's al Ghūl was planning to do next, the Dynamic Duo would be ready.

Rā's al Ghūl

REAL NAME: Unknown

OCCUPATION: International Ecoterrorist

BASE: Varies

HEIGHT:
6 feet 5 inches

WEIGHT:
215 pounds

EYES:
Green

HAIR:
Gray and white

Rā's al Ghūl has lived for centuries. He has seen the world change over the years, but his beliefs stay the same. He is dedicated to restoring Earth to its original, pristine form. To achieve this goal, Rā's will do whatever it takes, even if that means wiping out all of humanity in the process. Rā's has a legion of followers, including his daughter, who would readily give their lives to see his dream become a reality. Expect Rā's to be guarded at all times by his personal bodyguard, Ubu.

G.C.P.D. GOTHAM CITY POLICE DEPARTMENT

- Rā's al Ghūl regularly bathes in the Lazarus Pits to maintain his youthfulness and prolong his life. When Rā's undergoes the process, he must be alone, for he becomes temporarily insane when he emerges from the Pits.

- Rā's al Ghūl has lived for countless years. He has amassed a wealth of knowledge during his lifetime. His longevity has allowed him to master many fighting disciplines as well, making him extremely dangerous.

- Talia, Rā's al Ghūl's daughter, is a firm believer in her father's cause, and she would do anything to help. But Talia has feelings for the Dark Knight, which often conflicts with her responsibilities as Rā's al Ghūl's daughter.

- Rā's sees Batman as his equal, and he hopes to one day convince the Dark Knight to become husband to his daughter, Talia, and heir to his throne. In turn, Batman hopes to one day convince Rā's to help humanity rather than harm it.

CONFIDENTIAL

BIOGRAPHIES

Robert Greenberger began his career at Starlog Press where he created *Comics Scene*. Bob has also worked for both Marvel and DC Comics. He has written many *Star Trek* novels and short works of fiction, including *The Essential Batman Encyclopedia* and *Batman Vault*. He lives in Fairfield, Connecticut, with his wife, Deb, and their dog, Dixie.

Jason T. Kruse is an animation veteran of CalArts University in sunny California. He is the creator of the comic book *The World of Quest*, and he is excited to see its TV show air internationally later this year. Jason has worked as an animator on the films *Stuart Little, Cats and Dogs,* and *The Barnyard*. He has also worked on video games including *Star Trek: Tactical Assault, Master of Orion 3, Cashflow 101* and *Cashflow 202, Ratatouille,* and *Food Frenzy*.

Lee Loughridge has been working in comics for more than 14 years. He currently lives in sunny California in a tent on the beach.

GLOSSARY

adjusted (uh-JUHST-id)—moved or changed something slightly

buoy (BOO-ee)—a floating marker in the water

chain reaction (CHAYN re-AK-shuhn)—a series of events where each event leads directly to the next

desolate (DESS-uh-luht)—deserted and uninhabited

insulated (IN-suh-lay-tid)—covered something with material to stop heat from escaping

pristine (priss-TEEN)—a pure, unpolluted state

remote (ri-MOHT)—far away, isolated, or distant

sophisticated (suh-FISS-tuh-kay-tid)—clever or complex

threaten (THRET-uhn)—put something in danger

Utility Belt (yoo-TIL-uh-tee BELT)—Batman's belt, which holds all of his weaponry and gadgets

villain (VIL-uhn)—an evil or wicked person

DISCUSSION QUESTIONS

1. Rā's al Ghūl has lived for centuries by bathing in the Lazarus Pits. Would you want to live forever? Why might eternal life be a bad thing?

2. Batman and Rā's al Ghūl argued about their beliefs, but it didn't solve anything. Can good things ever come from arguments?

WRITING PROMPTS

1. Batman's beliefs conflicted with Rā's al Ghūl's beliefs in this story. Have you ever disagreed with someone? What did you argue about? Did your opinion change? Write about your argument.

2. Write your own story about Batman and Rā's al Ghūl. What evil plan does Rā's have in store for the Dark Knight? How will Batman fight the super-villain? You decide.

3. Both Batman and Robin were concerned about global warming, the greenhouse effect, and other threats to the environment. What are some things that we can do to help protect Earth?

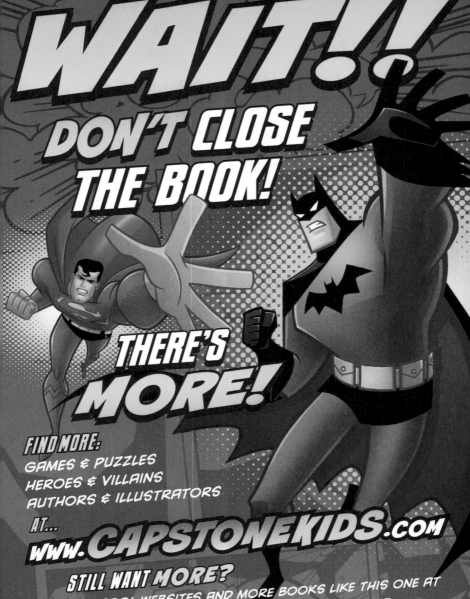

MORE NEW BATMAN ADVENTURES!

THE MAN BEHIND THE MASK

CATWOMAN'S CLASSROOM OF CLAWS

HARLEY QUINN'S SHOCKING SURPRISE

MY FROZEN VALENTINE

THE PUPPET MASTER'S REVENGE